THE MAN IN THE SCOTTISH

LUNATIC ASYLUM

A satirical comedy on the occasion of the Scottish referendum, Sept 2014.

by

DEDWYDD JONES

For Karl !

from

Dedwydd.

(Centre stage, lectern, shelves inside, with brochures; by lectern, standing bookshelves, table, scattered with brochures of Scotland, replica of the Declaration of Arbroath pinned up; documents in envelopes, piles of cuttings, medical reports on our lunatic, ALLY MacNALLY of the clan ALLY MacNALLY; all in disorder; behind table, screens, pinned up famous scenes, ruined castles, Abbeys, lochs, Bonnie prince Charlie, Flora MacDonald; big map of Scotland; ALLY uses pointer throughout, getting pictures mixed. ALLY talks in different accents; when he wishes to appear 'normal,' he talks with a less pronounced Scottish accent.

Facing audience are tourist 'gift boxes,' sides open, contents visible; tawdry tourist trinkets: plastic hand-flags of tartans, saltires pasted onto everything; golf balls in egg cartons, mini bottles of whisky; claymores; dirks, buckled shoes; miniature replicas of the stone of Scone, with bits of tartan; plastic thrones of Scotland, plastic William Wallace with spider; mini quails, pheasants, flying salmon, teeny Tam O'Shanters, haggises, tartan toilet rolls, huge conch shell (through which ALLY communicates with 'the other side' and the voices of the ancestors); carries a mobile; note-book, from which he sometimes quotes; untidy piles of torn, holed Highland dress, broken regalia; a saltire flag, furled on floor, only unfurled at end of play. ALLY dresses himself from time to time, until at end looks like a tramp in tartan rags; ALLY in saltire underpants, soiled frilled shirt, frantically searching through documents and brochures. Pauses and puts on tartan socks. Takes pills; Scratches himself, finds a flea, examines it. Does a frantic sword dance; drinks from carafe of water (laced with white whisky); sings snatch of 'Keep right on to the end of the road...' Stops, rummages; picks up pointer, looks around, approaches audience, noticing them for the first time)

ALLY *(Of audience):* So there ye are! *(Gestures to brochures)* I am Ally MacNally of the clan Ally MacNally *(repeats name in broad Scots accent, American and Irish accents, confused)* Now, permit me to present Scotland the Brave to you. *(Bows. Off stage, roars of rage, shouts, shots, jeers, chains clank, steel doors clang. Shouted orders, ' Raus! Raus!Raus!' Clash of arms. Stuka dives bombers, explosions; ALLY ignores noise, pounces on brochures, flourishes one. Cut sounds, ALLY reads)* I see! I see! I see there are thirty-four genus of fleas and midges in this pretty land of ours, and at the moment they all seem to be feasting on my flesh, from pit arms to further down too. They ought to introduce legislation against all fleas. They're a plant, of course. *(Scratches wildly. Sings a snatch of 'Keep on going to the end of the road...'Picks up envelope)* O my Doc, my Doc's final, finicky report once again, is it?! *(Reads)* '...challenging behaviour of patient Ally MacNally of clan Ally MacNally, me naturally, 'in the cell of a Rest Home' which is 'a model of care, in the splendid suburbs of Edinburgh...' Is it? Are they? Am I? They locked me in here, so I will lock myself out. No stools about that! I have a plan, in fact, hidden in hindsight. 'I gotta get outta this place…' *(Waves notebook)* I have it all noted down.

(Looks at watch. Off stage, roars of rage, shouts, shots, jeers, chains clank, steel doors clang; shouted orders, 'Raus! Raus! Raus!' Stuka dive bombers; ALLY listens, EXITS. Sound of smashing, crashing off stage. Clash of arms. ALLY RE-ENTERS, dusting hands)

ALLY: I am not the one who is undone, even though the door is furiously barred against me. And thrown away, no doubt, not the key, but me. They think. No brainers! Cure alls? Balls alls. *(Looks upward, sings)* 'It's alright Ma - life and life only.' And it's nearly time for my message. *(Looks at watch)* I always deliver my messages to the world right here at 7.30 prompt, come what bloody mayhem. They sometimes fall on me, fists flailing when they can see a message coming on but not today, I've just super-glued the locks with a hammer. *(Blows on conch-shell. Listens, nods)* Still in the tidal fogs, ancestors awaiting their movement orders. *(Seizes document)* But the doctor's crazy reports here. *(Reads out, laughing, tittering, guffawing, chortling)* "Ally MacNally of clan Ally MacNally,' well, well! '…this patient's 'non-verbal spatial linguistic abilities are riddled with paradoxa and psychomotor seizures,' causing 'vocal-auditory stoppages and a reluctance to return to normalcy, indicating decay of the left cerebellum between the chorea and the manea, the antique thalamus and the hypothalmus, the entire system of the frontal curvature, in the missing link area, also exhibit major malfunctions, a condition which attracts the patient to spinning entities, 'wheee! Wheee!' and to the 'too muchness' of things, especially where the instinctual determinants are concerned." *(Pauses)* And **I'm** in here?! Well, well. No, not well, not so well. Well, so what? But no, all my glorious brochures here prove the very opposite of these enigmatical incorporeal afflictions hanging in a void, inchoate to a man! No, I am not a sight! *(To audience)* All we need is a coffin to make us look really ridiculous, isn't it? *(Pause)* But I don't see any volunteers.

(Scots accent) I continuously adore brochures all over the land, see how I can't stop fingering them. Only a few of us do. But I do. I am not unquestionably ill in any way or stretch of the imagination, as my adoration of these lively glossies proves. I think brochures are the holy grail of the true Scotia, the original Albans, demonstrating Wittgenstein's socio-fiscal synthesis, 'tourists are good for you,' so warm-hearted and so saving, God help us! Yes, see, here, every good Scot believes what he has in his brochures for breakfast. Brochures are the modern day scriptures - and a Scotsman's best friend. And these pics here. See. I was there and there and everywhere. In the shades with the ancestors, I had reincarnations by the score and second sights too, more and more – first sight, second sight, third right on to the end. I get messages. The ancestors demand it. I mean, who else is there? Listen to the sea-spray in my hair! *(Blows on conch. Listens, scratches)* No. Out with the dolphins at play today. Lightning again. Yes, yesterday, in a vision, I saw all our

history laid out before me like one huge, endless roll of double-absorbent toilet tissue. So comfy - one thing I'll never change. I do a spin! *(Spins and dances)* No! Damn, I forgot, the PM! *(Dials on mobile, in Scots)* Hello, Downing St, number ten? Good, is that the Prime Minister of England. Good. Well here we are again, Prime One, let me begin my message this time. I just want to say how sorry I am again for being so independent before the year a.d. 1708 or nine or.... Yes, this is a formal public apology, quite out loud! To the populace in general Didn't do it on purpose. *(Listens, posh English)* And you are very sorry for the Union, too. *(Scots accent)* And I am sorry we ever had the four ancient independent Kingdoms, Pictland, Strathclyde, old Scotia... that lot. *(Listens. In English posh)* So you're sorry for yellow Hengest and Horsa too. Ochs to you. *(In Scots)* and I'm sorry that our first real success with divine right, King MacAlpine, reverted so badly to tribal points of view, all for himself. So sorry. *(Listens, sips drink, takes pill, English accent)* And you're sorry for our William the Lion's defeat at Alnwick, by the Hammer of the Scots, by the heavenly right of Yellowland, our First Teddy Plantagenet. What!? - you will! with Dunbar thrown in? And feelings of redemption for the kidnap of the Stone of Scone. So generous of you. Such self-effacement! Well, this deserves a really big one in return – this complete nation would like to apologise for the long spears of Braveheart at Bannockburn, but only as seen in the film. *(Listens)* Yes, every one of them. *(English posh)* As for the defeat of the Scots at Dunbar by the regicide Cromwell, forget it, not worth a 'sorry,' you are

7

not a man of constant sorrow. Cheer up! *(In Scots)* OK! Most of all, the man who nearly stood in the way of Scots progress, the Unbonnie Prince, what a Charlie! I do not apologise for that. *(Listens)* And you'll forget all about Culloden? Splendid wee fella. And forget about all the Highland Clearances, for delicious sheep, the Highlanders stripped bare, a magnificent sight. Mad John of the Red Bulls overturned by the primrose savages. Prestonpans but an illusion. Veu Victis! Spare the rod. You were right, we were wrong. Ma agreed. Or didn't agree, as the case may be. But note, there is a woman behind every article of wear, but at Braemer, Scots vestments were banned, the dear old Scots socks, the claymore too, and all yellow moving targets; the sporran out of sight, and the pipes and the kilt, nauseous alien mounds, we apologise for all of these P.M. *(Listens)* And you apologise right back for traducing them, and banning them, do you, caloo, callay, never thought they'd see the light of the Lays again! *(ALLY takes out sporran. Strokes it, scratches himself, examines a flea)* And now little sporran you are all mine, home again, not forgotten and forgiven, your little friends are waiting for you, one hop and you're away! *(Puts on sporran, scratches furiously)* "Constant sorrow?' Just expect tears as well as apologies from me, I am so sorry for you as much as I am for me. All part of some plan or other, somewhere. *(Into mobile)* And, PM, please convey my curtsies to their royal Altitudenesses, yes, of the Clan Humpty Dumpty, I believe, Hanover Mews! Tomorrow, who knows? Just beware the yellow ferals along the way! Och and away with ye!

(Roars of rage, etc, off stage, as before. ALLY EXITS, sounds fade to cries of terror. Sound of thumping, hammering. ALLY RE-ENTERS)

ALLY: I'm nailed in out there like a copulatory coffin, so I 're-arranged' the panels again. It's alright, Ma, just the agents of domestic powers, forget the foreign ones *(pointing at members of audience; in Scots)* you, you, you, all you bloody spy-faced yous, out there. I know who I am. I am himself, I am Ally MacNally of the Clan Ally MacNally, every last bit of me. Omelettes are scrambled, but not Ally's brains, which balance out to a 'T', I assure you. I exist only in the dreadful breakfast of my imagination, and that's a fact. I have been making up my mind in my head for generations. As for you out there, with your nutty deep-fried mars-bars, a plague of nits on the lot of ye! May your crotches seethe with microscopic reddish bites. And your armpits too, those disgusting otters, I'm not forgetting them nasty stink pits of yours either. Bottoms to the lot of you! I'm in here because I know. You're out there because you don't! Simple as that. *(ALLY listens at conch)* Yes, all messages accepted, Ma, but only if they come FROM Desolation Row! Bloody you, Ma, hell and night soil once more, my Lady, and that applies to any Yellow sated saboteurs and agent provocateurs out there as well. *(Listens)* L'enfer and latrine-seats! *(into conch)* - put the ancestors on red alert then, never mind if you do feel dry and lifeless after use! Whew! *(Picks up brochure, uses pointer)* Yesterday I was off to gentler lands, the Outer Hebrides, the Isle of Lewis where Floral

Macdonald helped her Prince standing on the argent strand, her arms outstretched, and had ...an... orgasm? Yes, no I think. No not that. She had *(consults brochure)* no, she had a 'vision', yes, that's it. Not the other. Not our Flora, the flower of Highland maidenheads with her Prince of Tam O'Shanters. Change the 'o', a silly alphabetical blunder. *(Pause)* I loved someone once too out there. Yes... Where...? *(Searches frantically, finds a glossy brochure, reads out, referring to map; Scots accent)*

Yes, Ma, I have to say as I watched the sunset from the Lynn of Lorn, it was first the sea, shining and flat and red, and the shore browned and flecked with white, to the green, sloping hills, and the blue Loch stretching inland to the mountains in the mists and then just before the close of day, the golden sun stood huge and waiting and then I heard the voices of the ancients there sweeping and singing over the tides, came to me on the heights, messages the first, not of 'union' but of 'unity,' exploded in my mind like a bolt of lightning and I fainted out of love and understanding of them and the still standing islands of life. It was then I knew I could not bear to lose one more inch or time of this Lynn of Lorn any more. I knew at once I would get out of the cell of this place and raise the flag again for them, the spirits of the vanished clansmen who fought so hard for us. I was their man. Out there. *(Blows on conch)*

(Scots accent) Yes! To the gritty-nitties - especially observe now, Glasgow, up here, called 'Weegieland', and Edinburgh, down there,

called 'Burgherland', the Highs versus the Lows - to think the Highs once called the Lows 'sassenachs,' the ultimate yellow provocative expletive, but behold them all - Dora's night creatures, the daylight robbers, wee nyafs by the score, weak antiquated wabbits, bampots, the red menacers, but, to avoid tribal confusion, I have put them all under one generic name, N-E-D-'s, who come from every rank, however malodorous, the infamous Non-Educated Delinquents, N-E-D's, from John O'Groats to Perth and Kinross, I'm pretty sure! Enjoying your first brush with the N.E.D's, are you? And the right altar boys are on the right hand side of God hisself, and the left ones on the left hand side of exactly the same god hisself, but at each other's throats, night and day, the Sniffies versus the Prodies, the Blue Noses versus the Left Footers, the Jam Tarts versus the Hibbers, even the turncoats, the cream of the South Britons - the amber scourge - versus bloody well everybody - more monuments, I say, for the gift boxes, more healing phials of MacBeth spring water, what cures - Awe Loch Awe - more of Fingall's Marmalade, and lots of messages from Ossian on the Isle of Egg. Raise the banner! Oh, those darling nurse boats! How I wish one would glide along now for you and me, and the Burghers and Weegies to adore. But forward ye Albans, headed by the Burghers, foremost...for...

'...Edinburgh is the Athens of the North!

Brodgar, the Pompei of the North,

Egilsay, the Egypt of the North,

Badenach, the Neptune of the North,

Braham Seer, the Nostradamus of the North,

Hanover Square, the Harrods of the North,

Dundee, the Naples of the North,

Glasgweegie, the Venetian Blinds of the North,

Templeton's old carpet factory, the Doge's Palace of the North, Hadrian's Wall, south of the north, the Land of the Yellow Anuses.

So - *(Holds up a skeleton costume; in broad Scots)* skeleton costumes for all our dead heroes in shop windows I say! And, look, *(Holds up box of props)* these precious mementoes, straight from the new brochure-maisons of Weegie and Burgher, the tartan eggs, the saltire soap, the weeny pale haggises, and - a good one here, *(swings stone on end of string)* a tiny stone of scone, with bits of Macdonald tartan hanging on, like skin off a Yellow corpse. Bless our clan boutiques and oat-filled basements, why, *(of brochures)* with these behind us, we can't go wrong, can we? – go Forth to Firth, young man! Gaze from the double canti-levered celebration of rust, or bridge, see the many paddle-steamers of great pleasure paddling about… and, I kid you not, another gift box here - more tartan thimbles, condoms, dildos, Harry Lauder lavender trews, flies undone, cold pipes, hot drones, big cabers, with tartan ducks, here Burghers putting the hammer, tossing the shot, whole lot of Highland flinging going on. And, look, Willwall with his friendly little spider, in real lead. I mean that, no I do not. I do not think so, I do! I saw the Sun God, Lugh, naked in torchlight at the Marymass Fair; an ancient Scots fiddler burst out of the bushes covered with burs from burdock, riding a Clydesdale cart horse, waving his dirk at the tartan God. I felled the traitor with a single painted stone from the Isle of Lewis. Mock a Scot? Never. I call for independence. No I don't. I mean look at it this way. *(Drinks, takes pill, in posh Scots)* If we were independent we would be at liberty to admit we do drunkenness brilliantly all by ourselves without subsidies from the southern Yellow Folks, that our electric cocktails are of our own making, that all the pukers and knee-tremblers along the Royal Milestone are ours, out of our honey-dew factories and lobster shacks. Admit that, or refuse to, and you're soon a loon and join me here. No, no jobs. An old trap. I refuse to admit I can do that by meself. It is the tertiary ruffians over the border that make me so lazy. If I get one, what would I do without it. Work? Ugh no, perish that. That's what would happen to take the responsibility for Jocks having jobs for ourselves, and with even our own Scottish character, without any kind of apology?! Them themselves!? No scapegoats, no Yellow bottle openers?! Take responsibility for our own hard-ons? Just us? What high-handedness! It's all a filthy plot. Ma said that. I have it noted. 'Be yourself.' She is confused by me, not me of her. Listen to her, and I mean everywhere! She was present at the Highland Clearances, every one of them. A little old toughy, she blanched at the hairy legs, the twisted lips, slack jaws, the bulging sporrans, the foul claymore - "what primordial Pictish swine!" she shrieked, "who let this lot out? I thought these low Highlanders had been kept secret in our scarlet bogs for untold centuries." But undimmed, she danced a gay jig in the byre of her Dad's MacDonald Clan, while her mother's family came from the dreadnoughts of the custard-coloured people, and could only dance the yellow horn-pipe, the turnskirts! More of a touch of the tarburgh about her.

Well, I myself danced no paean of triumph. I didn't mean it. That's what would happen again with independence, it would mean another plague of Highland Giants, another hairy Diaspora! And endless oil slicks. Bless you, Ma, you got their measure back and front, cut them off without a sporran, in spittle of your past. *(Aside, to audience)* My Ma, by the by, was also a handmaid champion of the sex trade, just opposite the Scott Memorial - ' Dora's Dollalhambra,' it was called, the Sherehezade of the cat- houses of the north, where Dora had assembled the most tasty tarts of the Cairngorms, and beyond. Dora's throbbing helpers were legion, spectacular and original. Her sex-workers were divided into squads, magisterial makers of the beast with three backs, with fresh hand-job specialists, youthful masturbatory associates, climax supervisors, suck Tsars, anal auxiliaries, majordomo flagelants, minor directresses of fellatio, back-up cunnilinguans, transvestitan sponsors, Task Force Dominatrexes, 'pornocracy at its best', she proclaimed proudly to the world, Pictland's proudest Madame. But she would never have achieved global distinction were it not for her piece de resistance. After years of mass copulation and the minutiae of multiple fornication, she launched it - a pulsating perpetually revolving vagina! Yes. It never stopped. A few turns, and you were in outer space, whee, whee, wheeeee!! Dora became Queen of the Come Machine, and went on to conquer nation after nation until they became so exhausted they fell into the sleep of peace, something never achieved before or since by any global power on earth. Yes. Scotland's own Queen Dora, my darling, spun herself into immortality virtually everywhere, the egg on the top of the age of Scottish Enlightenment!

(Picks up a brochure. Notices audience) Hello there, lovely tall tourists, you follow me now, full purses at the ready or something, just joking. Welcome, as I continue to present the real Alba, Latin for Bonny Scotland, brimming with tartan feats and reels! Look! What another brochure is this! *(Reads out)* Hey, listen, in anno domine 185, the big Tribune, Agricola, entered Aberdeenshire, and know what he did then? ran off before the purplish hords of Picts and hid behind Hadrian's Wall. That Roman from Rome scaled the very depths of pusillanimity, and when his mate Antoninus came to help, he lost his entire ninth Legion in the waters of the Minge Thus was the Curse of Caledonia born, the

terrors which tamed Tacitus! - this at a time when the Nurses had colonised the Inner Hebrides, happy day, calloo callay, the relief of the Clans was palpable! Meanwhile, Stirling Castle, where the boxwood parterres are in the shape of a vast crown, where every crook and nanny is crammed with history, where, to soften the blow, twee-twee lapwing chicks are on display in their nests, and, for a small extra charge, the Dance of the Tartan Teddies will send you on your way somehow profoundly comforted. Then the potato harvest failed in the Heights. Victoria bought Balmoral for its precious spuds, and ten percent of the population emigrated, but no worry, the departed were mere remnants of the vassals and villeins of the humbled thicko Feudal Red Wig shakers. I should know. I was there too, all over as I said. But here, look at the Stones of Brodgar and Stenness, look carefully, see them, they are so thin, so very thin, are they not? Listen, wouldn't it just take an Englishman to try and starve a stone? But back to 'the auld enemy,' aka, the 'dandelion beasties,' Berwick changed hands those thirteen times until it got fed up with the surgery, and stopped. That was just where somewhere Robert the Bruce did his spider act for the ages. I saw him, I was the voice that urged him on, "climb, you spider, climb!" That was me. Then Eddie Two, a gay, why not, granted us our independence when we already had it, cheeky sod and the Pope agreed, the apostolic cocksucker, lot of spiritual dunces, deistic blockheads around. I was there. They simply would not listen. Ma went ecstatic. *(Aside)* Not a 'Ma' really, a male woman, in trousers and panties, what's wrong with that? I never denigrate, even ridicule, a dyke, beyond the pale, I never even use the word. She's a bi-sexualist extraordinaire, and nothing wrong with that, married to the Kirk, Calvinism kept her decent, and we only had group sex on Saturdays, feeling up OK on the Sabbath but only before manual consummation came off. You can't deride her/him for that. I don't mean to be offensive to any one, except perhaps the offensive. I mean fair's fair to all the two-nippled ones, I mean, us, generally, and if there are any triple-nippled ones out there, human rights for them too! It's alright Ma, nothing to say sorry for, and I'm not going to say sorry for that even at holy Kildulton Cross, the Celtic one, to beg for more or less. *(Consults notebook)* Yes, another historical note. *Yes,* in modern times, in 1999, the Burghers of Dun Edin went capital and its population went posh. See, in the old tenements, the toffs lived on the upper floors so they could throw their piss pots down onto the hoi polloi, who lived on the lower floors, so the so-called gentry, seeing there was only a shitty future for them, piled all their expensive goods and chattels on the pavement, which drove the lower Burghers wild, because they possessed none of these luxuries and began a little quiet pillaging. But the piss-pot throwers made it to the suburbs in the new towers built about 1750 or so, to commemorate, on their knees, the kinda Prussian-type Fuhrer-monarchs who were not dead yet, plastering crescents, circles and squares with the names of the chinless Hanoverians, the 'Fredericks,' the 'Charlottes', the 'Georges,' sort of thing, by divine as well as royal right, of course.

Yes, Clearences, thank goodness, came back into fashion. The marvellous Strathnaver one in 1819 AD, was tops - a place denuded by fire, purified by flame, black as pitch - und Alban-frei! Ma was ecstatic. 'No more Wooly Mammoths,' she shouted to all her nurse girlfriends. One sniff of royal Balmoral and she soon showed her true colours. Yes, the Fields of the Cloth of Gold of the lurking Ex- Pats and present canary Yellows, had come - the vast Sporting estates of hunting, riding and fishing fame, the hard pursuit of the red deer, the dull Scottish fields and pastures stamped out under foot. Spies, agitators, radicals, reformers, infiltrators, pincoes, and nationalists all chucked into the duck ponds of the new jaunatre dispensation, and a law introduced to promote all acts of subservience, both Burgher, Weegie and NED's, and others of that ilk, indefinable but unmistakable! But it never quite took root. Just riots and loads more drunks. *(Waves brochure, sips drink, takes pill, grimaces)* Before us now spread over twenty-thousand heather-savannahs, crammed with strutting pheasants and the humble quail, 20,000 per hour, and all dead! The rights of all owners of the new Fatalism were at once respected. I mean, over 150,000 Scots died for the fell Yellows in the First World War. There's respect for you. We had finally become one vast branch factory, with new shop colonies, the Tesco Protectorates, for example, and the like, – which will never shut, like the grave. Hilarious, yes? What could Independence do about that even if it was close by? Why, brush it all under the carpets and dance a reel on the grave of hard work. Bless our great Afghan Involvement, may the Highlanders and Lowlanders, thick and thin, rest in the comradeship of interment, the dustbins of peace-loving Buttercups everywhere, thank god! Our skeleton heroes are not alone over there, ye know, the gravestones stretch over the horizon! The Trump of Doom is a fine capital too! *(Finds a brochure. Reads it)*

Back to the Burghers, it says, origin of, 'the borough of 'Eden', or 'Edin,' or Edinburgh, of divine origin, was built on hills, four hills and a half, to be exact, the Rome of the North - and a half. This includes the mountainous King Arthur's Seat, filched millennia ago from the swilling Taffs far below. And the Burghers deserved it, they had been harried in 1174,1296,1313,1357,1473,1650,-bang, bang, bang, bang! - so many sulphurous skirmishes, confrontations, raids, envelopments, of both flanks, gorgeous! - bombardments, sieges, hairy heads on poles up to and not beyond 1689, to name but a few. And let it be said, the levelling of the Premontean Abbey of Dryberg was a relief, if you ask me, bugger the Augustinians, the Irenians and the Cistercians and those silly rose windows of Roslyn, with their futile mystical emblems, put them aside. They are not native. Remember, the Ally of MacFayed is Laird of 65,000 grass-roots pheasantries and countless acres, not far from Sweetheart Abbey, where Carlyle was born, a little on the far side of the soggy wetlands, I admit, at the tip of the hornèd moon. But some said the fairies had exchanged him for a ripe pedant. But his pedantry, I believe, was exaggerated. You can never trust these apoplectic wire-heads, though I do just that to test out the ferocious moles and turncoats among them, and us, so to speak, as well. Watch your backs, is the watchword, and your daughters too, their fronts. Yes. No more mothers of all wars, whores and confusions.

Yes, but whatever the batterings, the hammerings, the harryings, the drunkenness, the darling Union Act stopped the Burgers and Weegies, the despicable NED's, in their tracks and they have been wonderfully servile ever since. Bless'd subservience! What a relief! Up those old begging cups! Nothing like empty bowls to encourage a hundred thousand crawlers or two, to your side.

Meanwhile, here, Our Lady of Glasweegie, City of Culture and Darts, with her broken silhouettes and fallen masonry, her ground-floor Housing Projects, she could still boast of noisome drains, poisonous effluvia, choking emissions, open air cloacas, super middens, fine outbreaks of rickets, cholera, small pox, diptheria, leavened with alcoholism and crack, with Highlanders fighting the Ulstermen on every manhole cover - ah, the good old days! But 'rat fear is not cured by magic dentures.' Thank you, Doc! But the Pheasant-mad Yellows still pursued the poor Pictish fowls to their north, or was it south? This from a Firth which had given the great battleships, the Howe, the Indefategableubble, the Vanguard to the war crimes commission, were now tossed aside like a soiled glove - the city which had donated 180,000 shell fuses to Flanders Field in a single week-end. How the khaki unknowns in their mausoleums gave three cheers for democracy! But the herring- boat fleets were drowned in the backwash of blood, yet the haggises, thank God, remained afloat and were towed inshore to the clamorous tourist crab-counters on the jetties. But note cunning Aberdeen in all this. Listen. The actual U.S. Land and Cattle Company was run from Aberdeen. It was the canny Aberdonians who opened up the West! California or bust! Hudson Bay too. I saw it all. That cattle company prospered with the aid of the pistols of Butch Cassidy, which this far-sighted company had employed, to add to the legend of Scotland the Brave everybloodywhere. And the hyperbolic Nuclear power stations were run down and out! In a final salute, the ghost of skin-covered St Columba sailed in his round coracle up the straits, where three deep-water lochs meet – SPLASH! and gave the sign of the cross, a gesture which endures to this day *(Searches for brochures)* somewhere.

Which reminds me, I always wanted to do a cow poke. *(Imitates cowboy)* Listen, pardners, the Stone of Destiny was finally re-stolen, with a lasoo, and repatriated. Was I present!? I was that lasoo! And what happened then, Gosh, man, the Revenge of the Marigold Mob – yes, the era of the Great Indifference set in: the Steel Mill of Gartcrosh was locked out, the Car Works of Lindon were abandoned, the Pulp Mill of Fort William ignored, the Truck Plant at Bathgate, removed; the coal fields at one stroke and the Clyde at two. Thus the Yellow Brooms prospered after all. But all those closures would have been catastrophic with Independence on our door step. Poor old Weegies and their holed dinghies. And what about the gargle-and plum-speaking, pinny-wearing, limp-wristed Burghers? They knew they could feed breasts in public without being prosecuted on Sundays, or pay the fees of their molly-coddled, feeble, strangulated offspring lolling idly in their squalid parks. Student wasters everyone. And is this not correct? *(Consults note-book)* John of Fordun was a chronicler from an antique land and he wrote, "the Lowlanders are urbane, trusty, patient, affable, and peaceful." Ma was beside herself with agreement. And it's me who's supposed to be distracted by distractions *(Reads in female voice)* - "They were never effeminate," - that's Ma all over - "they merely move along the pavement like flowers in a May breeze, even when they cross the road. So natural. And they only speak Lallands because there is no other." "Huh," I put the knife in, "you think you're posh now, don't you, just because you had a wank in Edinburgh!" How she huffed and puffed! Then, I have it word for word, she had another go at the Highlanders, any 'landers 'by now, it seems, listen! - "savage, untamed, rude, much given to rapine, pillage and exceedingly cruel to the Yellows when night falls," which was OK with the majority I told her ! Ssh, Ma. I agree some of the time, but very discreetly," I warned her, "but let me get my hiss in too – I too was there, don't forget – and to be frank, there was rotten stuff going on, yes, *(Reads from notebook)* it's true 'they do dwell in baleful industrial dustbins, always under the influence of ardent spirits and speak Gaelic because there is no other. And they have invented sort of costume clothes, all silly I agree, - worst jackets, Prince Charles Coatees, silver mounted sporrans, lace jabots, silk cuffs, gillie shoes, chequered hose, doublet shined, and a war bonnet with a white feather, and a sprig of heather, the very blossom everyone is sick and tired of seeing, and an acre of off-the-colour-spectrum tartan over the shoulder! What whoppers! I can be furious too. They sit outside their peat-bog huts with their perpetual begging bowls at their feet. What monstrous fakes, 'why,' my condemnation now, 'these new BBB's, these high and dry Bed and Breakfasters, even have honeyed words for the Forked-tongue Ones, the old Etonian legion this time, unforgivable, and that caused further outbreaks of criss-cross coloured cloths. All over the Low part of the Highlands and the High part of the Lowlands, Victoria on the side, smothered in clan-chiefs' shades! That's it, Ma, exit, svp, goodnight! The relief of Ally MacNally! How those new-born colours spread! Tartan now all over even more inert trinkets; tartan tea cosies, tartan rubbers, condoms, dildoes, vibrators by the score along the Bordel Mile, shiver me timbers! - especially when Dora was Queen! I read my very words, Ma. But the lavatorial Yellows never surfeited, called for more, still more. Every Scots cat now has its own tartan, and this avalanche of pussy adornment has spread far and wide. 'Be one with Balmoral' is the name of the game and it drives the monarchists to true-blue sartorial ecstasies, wedded to the most unconstrained reels and routs going, like the World Pipe Band Championship, from Pole to Pole. What a conspiracy! There are pipe bands in Istanbul from Kent, Samurai sword dancers from Hiroshima in Kensington, all swirling away. They play at the same hour at Hogmanay, the little Xmas, the 'the Wee Cooper o' Fife' of Robbie the Burns, spot on Greenwich Mean Time - tick-bloody clock! And there are 600 Highland Games going on somewhere all over the universe. Braemar pulls in only twenty thousand per day, but the USA pulls in 250,000 per event! Heaving the haggis has achieved ludicrous heights - across the Potomac it went recently, 'hurled by an inflamed American matron' and it was converted into Olympic gold. What a Highland fling! The Grampians reel! I made, man, like a stag with Antlers. Brought the house down! And the blazing Fiddles Competition wowed them in Washington DC! Listen, it was all due to those lumpy, dread-locked, exported Aboriginals of ours. They did all this on purpose. They had no dead quails or pheasants to offer at the knees of the gastronomic Yellows, until their roots were cleansed. The Grand Tartan Conspiracy! And I alone am in a position to know all about it. I just told you, Ma – Ally me! *(Puts note-book away)* And let me tell you, when the towering Hairies want war, they go to Glasgow on a Saturday night. A word of warning to all - they are not bauchie but they are definitely heidbangers, devotees, to a man, of all the wee goldies in the land. As to God, I think the Burghers have it and so do the Weegies. You stand in a field in Edinburgh to be closer to your Maker, you bow your head to trees, you do not grovel on your knees. The Weegies gulp blood from that monotheistic everlasting corpse of theirs, but, come on now, we all worship the same Saviour like mad, do we not? We all clamber up the same bloody Romano-Jewish poles. We all nailed him, didn't we? We all did, really, for we are all equal in the Guys of Odd. *(Aside)* And, listen to me, by stools and sexual intercourse, if you dare deny me, I'll smash your immemorial guilt to a bloody pulp and your relatives too!) And my qualifications for these hard, heady hits are irresistible - I beat Zwingli hollow at Transubstantiation, thrashed Calvin on Papal infallibility, trounced the Carpenters with Hammer and Nails! Just en passant. Above all, see humility as a joke! bottom of the poubelle! - how I've learned about the eternal verities in here! Ssh! Deaf and dumb agents reported I'd been spying on the nuclear detergent, the Forth's first yellow submarine, called 'Astute,' but 'prostitute' seems more fitting to me, and accused me of incester worship with my sister in the glens and soldering workshops of the five Ports. That's what I have to put up with here. But this, a note of sylvan serenity now, Rothiemurgus forest hasn't changed in thirty thousand years, ferns and lichen still grow from its dripping granite blocks. And every day, a great new pastime, Water Golf is now played in the gulf, with its lines of liquid holes, a pretty sight, and I mean just that. No tight-arsed stuff. I mean it. Ask Ma, she's flying low tonight. *(Finds a brochure)* Ah, yes! 'Let them drink Drambuie', Dame Dora declared, 'after every climactic event.' Why not, cheap as pee after pots of curry, but with what outcome? The Weegie Streets are paved with vomit, while in Burgherland the vomit is paved with streets. Pongs whichever way you look at it, in spite of the MacAdam, bless him. Moreover I still cannot get used to footbridges swaying at 2,000 feet above ancient Lanark shell-holes, as a tourist thrill. Ugh!

And look at what else came out of the great universal Drambuie Binge, you would not believe it, fruits of fabulous genius, all born locally: long logarithms, small carbon dioxide atoms, high geological temperatures, towering names for the ages! – Tom Clerk, Maxwell Hutton, Gordon Ramsay, John Paul, Carnegie Jones, Fleming Zeno, 'who all radiate their glow far beyond the borders of their native lochs and terns.' And this is not to mention Doyle Stevenson, Rawling Burns, Scott Hogg, the divine MacGonnegal, even when down to his last pentameter, and this above all, the Sagas of Ossian, beloved of Napoleon Bonaparte!

(Takes out note book) I heard this in a pub at nine this morning, dialogue between a Low One and a High One! *(Reads)*

"What you havin?"

"Mine's a high ball-Knox with a twist of lemon. What's yours?"

"I'm havin' a double Cardinal, shaken not stirred. What you havin' next?"

"A Calvin Rainbow with all the trimmin's. What you havin'?"

"A triple Zwingli, with angostura bitters."

What harmony reigned, brotherhood herself, with only the sounds of gulping to keep the record straight, there was once peace in our time!

They went on - "But help me here, this old newspaper scandal, here *(reads)* "Plebgate, the scandal...pleb...what is a 'pleb?'"

"In Yellowland or in Scotland?"

"Both."

"OK. In Yellowland, it means a type of the lowest order of class, verging on their dandelion untouchables, like traffic wardens."

"So, what 's a 'pleb' in Scotland then?"

"Why...I think, it's ...LATIN!"

That's the kind of wonderful dialogue you hear on the highways and lowways, here and there. So, of course, Kultur Kreig broke out again. The Weegies were raw and exuberant, the 'Glasgow Boys', an old term, they were called, poor little simians, and went abroad to paint Sunset Boulevard with all the French top daubers in 'the auld ally,' Paris. While the Lows, the dastards, foully wooed the perfidious Yellows and Mr Raeburn became the most royal painter at the Court of the Jauniced Ones, the little piglet, and was knighted with that nasty snake-like rapier of the third Jasmine Monarch. And Mr Raeburn fell for it! Rise he did, Sir Yellow Ponce! Traitor to Tartan till the end of time! Bless our Pictish stone- carvings, I say!

I returned to my lovely Clan-gathering, my much more trustworthy 'oatmeal Olympic' club. It opened with a lone piper. I was that lone piper. And a forty-seven whistle band. I was those tin whistles. I won the tug of war against all comers. And it was me, not King Malcom Canmore in 1054 who won the first sword dance ever, although he was a legend in his own toilet, it was yours truly, spinning again, reincarnations incarnate! And the caber? A gigantic heave and up it went, right on twelve o'clock, and came down with a terrific thump, upright in the mud, stuck forever, a fine solitary standing monument for the ages. Still of me, I have a sketch of it, and on view for a small extra charge. Oh, the greens of the Gordons, the whites of the Cotton Pickers. Then to the home visits on Hogmannay with its salts and coals, to ward off evil spirits, like the Revenue and the Yellows. Then the Burning of the Clavie, an old saffron-coated assistant-hangman sort of fellow, plunged into a tar of flaming barrel, just as a warning. Then the Riding of the Marches, the Casting of the Colours, a sentimental trip really, to visit all the places burned to the ground by both High and Low, our very own scorched earth policy, where Yellow territory begins. What Beltanes of Dire Devils were there, what pageants of slaughter, what Maggie pograms, what Tory hecatombs, why even the non-pagan Sun God Lugh was present, he nodded to me in a most gracious and familiar manner as he passed. Remember, it was only the golden hoard in the diplomatic pouch that did for us. But not for long. I was not there. You'll see. And then King Malcom came clean about '*the* game', it was when he was disguised as a shepherd, he spotted a cowherd with a bit of stick hitting sheep droppings into the mouth of a rabbit hole. That was it. His admission was perfect. He ordered his wise men and deepest seers to improve on it and they came up with it, 'Golf!" they shouted smashing at the animal night-soil with long-shafted sticks, - and created 567 huge links on the spot, 'the Sport of Perfect Balls,' he called it. Good old brawny, tawny Malcom! So right, in spite of his colouration! He turned to his gillie who was crawling over peat and through heather, on his belly, stalking the 'beats', havens of the deer, a proud and happy fugitive of the Clearances. He could hit a red deer stone dead from the top of a Scots pine. Trump that! And then, the Water Golf! Bless our blessings! There. Feel better now, enlightened by my enlightenment? Golf leaves no doubt about it at all. Let me see. *(Consults notes)*

The Vatican actually believes in all this, and will not ride roughshod over any part of it, however overtly fiery the Weegies are. We will take care of the fleas on the Lord's right hand as we promised. After all, the Victual Provider of the Papal See, brought 17,000 bottles of Glenlivet alone last year. More Drambuie was dispatched to the starving investment brokers of Kenya, more than ever before, aquavitae for future generations of malarials. What charity! There are over two and a half thousand brands, understand, the Holy See finally had to appoint a large number of whisky tasters to aid the Victual Provider, a very Christian act, performed by the pious Cardinal Alex MacKardini of Firenze, but, listen to this, born in Firenze, perhaps, but conceived in *Inverness*. Drams from the Highland stills never drove the faithful blind, it just made them fighting mad. Their antique copper stills are still terrific at Speyside's Whisky Festivals. But what to eat with the honey dew? Porridge by the ton, haggis by the barrel loads; 'smokies,' smoked kippers, heaven sent; flat tatties, peeled potatoes; piles of neeps; sheep's stomach, lamb's bladder; pigs snout, rabbit heids, brie-crab-scuttles, and to top it off, a kittle, a kind of little sweet. If we do not kill them in battle we will kill them at table.

When I mentioned these urgent, immemorial questions to Ma, she merely put her foot down, "don't make me think, it's far too painful!" "Think anciently," I urged her in response, "think antiquarianously, think of things former and daft, and you'll be with me in here soon enough waving the flag of Saltire sanity, with gay laughter in the wings." She humphed and mumphed, and retired to her bedchamber, but came to the right conclusion in the end, although she was covered with blood, like most people who vote the right way! The next moment, she confided to me that darling Dora had wisely remained horizontal about the whole movement to the super suburbs and prospered splendidly, especially during the interminable Wars of Theological Spats, and where are they now? Dora's back at the new Whisky Heritage Exchange, the Joy Centre

Annnex, the Writer's Hangover Rest Cubicles, what acumen! - where weary sex-workers and clapped-out wordsmiths enjoy low-pressure, sub-thermal, reclining meditation couches, the Rubbing Palace of Joy, a fall-back transept of Dora's Alhambra, very popular with week-end virgins, both male and female, soon fully restored. Ma had the touch. Eat your heart out, ye Weegies, the Burgers had her all! *(Scots accent)* As for Kultur, buckets of the stuff! At Crook Inn, hard by Jedburg, Burns wrote his 'Willie Whistle's Wife.' It is said in the taverns of the town that Shakespeare's last words were, "O, would that I had expired in brave old Jedburg." Over two and a half thousand crenellated and uncrenellated castles here and there, but the recruiters always beat their first retreat to the courageous village of Coldstream. How utterly murderous were the male inhabitants there, of all ages, not even an ant left standing on the pavement. But this did not prevent General Roundhead Monk's dirty army from sneaking up to Flodden Field like mobile gorse bushes in full bloom, where some 5,000 noble kneeling Presbyters died, and some, shame to tell, not even dead drunk. But is it true – we're only Scottish when the Yellows are breathing down our necks? *(Mobile rings)* Hello, yes. Still sorry about Flodden? Good. So am I. *(Closes mobile. Sips, grimaces, looks at drink, examines a pill. Becomes furious)* Double dung and inexpressible ordure, who put water in my Glenlivet? And these pills – they've got placebo written all over them! *(Looks into audience)* Who..? you bloody 'yous' out there. Set the ancestors on you I will. My revenge...what I'll do, I'm not sure yet, but it'll be the terror of the shires. No, not true, I know exactly what to do, ye flannelled fools with your varnished stumps, you will be done for by my plan, and it will be in sight of Culzean Castle, the holy spot where the Virgin wed her Guy. That alone justifies the Union, if anything does. You wait! But before you move on, don't forget the General Ploughshare Museum, where Burns got the line 'wee timrous, cowering, beasties…' etc, etc. not on his bloody tractor. There's Poosie Nancy's Tavern, the Grey Mare's Tail, and as you look along the moors, up stands the great two-sworded master himself, not the spider man, but braw WW, Braveheart, in deep blue woad! There! Arghhh! Then Septimus Severus arrived and Antoninus built a wall for him, by hand, as I said. And still the Burgers, Weegies, NEDs and Hairies held their own genitalia on the ramparts, shaking them splendidly at dusk, Pictish victors over the barbarians and the bellowing Yellows on top. On the left, looms the Mull of Kintyre, trivialized by Sirrah Paul MacArtney! Just piss anywhere, that's what I do. Why did the Onanites of the One Beach so weep over Glencoe. *(into mobile)* And don't tell me the message from HQ didn't arrive in time. Bloody Last Post fable, their butcher Cumberland was there quick enough with his cleavers, and reduced the noble bloody crofters to dead corpses in a trice. The poor MacDonalds, all cut down and out. No revenge I say, just slay them bloody back, to a man! *(Holds up brochure)* Next time, hoist the magic flag of Dunegan Tower over the field, a guarantee of fertility, virginity and victory! It says. And do not forget to genuflect a bit to the little spiritual chapel outside the back vestry, made out of scrap-metal from the sunken ironclad hunships, style of Scapa Flow, and a chancel famous for its display of painted Stuart moustaches, row upon row, in oils; site of former Jacobite phantoms roving the cloisters in their typical coarse, white habits, praying for their Leader to return, pathetic remnant of loving Flora and… and it was a 'vision' she had, yes, not the other. Anyway, divine right down the drain. Yes… yes…well…well… It's alright…Lynn of Lorn is it? Ma? Yes…

(Finds brochure) And what about this immense floral clock in the Street of Princesses. 20,000 plants pushing two electric hands, I mean cruelty to green shoots and I'm no clock-watcher. And the Bankers built the Bank of Scotland in such a way that it would dissolve like salt at a later date with escape features built in everywhere. Next to Dora's, the Four-Inch Pillars of the Apprentices, and the Tantrum Centre. All got to begin somewhere. And lower down, Burns's Choragoric Monument of Lysicrates. Some quartiers were wasted by castration, or is it – deforestation? Never mind, and other heaths swallowed up by imported Cappadocian pines. Two-thousand snow leopards and twenty-seven albino rhinos were introduced, but did little to revive local flocks. But the investment breakers, the fouled, squinty-eyed managers, the footpad brokers, the discorporate lawyers and phony ice-cream vendors, did alright thank you, Jock. And then the Coming of the Festivals. What a one is the Burgher One! 'Why the City is the best place on earth to be,' as Shakesburt said again on the first birthday. I quote from the good

book of course. Fire-eaters, juggler-tumblers, high-flying clowns, jazz-infused strolling minstrels, miming fiddle players, general warblers, cram the pavements with money. Fifty million tickets a day and that's just for the outside! The Military Tatoo at the end of the day, all over the body. A Metropolis of one million paying guests! Forty-four mini copulative cornucopias every night, what about that! But all the fornications to be got through, unimaginubble! But the Weegies got their speaking person too, and about time, I say up the Weegies! 'the most beautifullest city ever built in the Union, forget the slums before and after it,' said a stunning Yellow Laureate, and 'a tremendous centre of hygiene now,' after all, Glasgow means a 'green, green place,' 'dear hidden beauty' in the Gaelic. So move over you big-headed, namby pamby Burghers! And up the road, the Permanent Vigil Hides for the Monster of the Loch, with tons of sightings, especially after the Whisky Tasters' Carnival. So much golden dew is drunk that even the dolphins are bottle-nosed! No apologies for that either. The Weegies fought and did retain their right to wash clothes on the city's greens, but gave it up because they could not tell the greens from the cabbage, and used public tap water somewhere. Bless St Mungo and his religious life! Nurse ships sailed past the Ivor Novello Building, and Betjman, the top bard of the Yellows declared insistently that the Weegie capital to be the 'greatest Victorian Thing in Europe.' The new Willow Tree Tea Rooms catered for many of the blue-rinse Hag Riders of the Skye – see, glimpses of enlightenment everywhere! And gape at the Weegies's Mercantile

Municipal Chambers, high on the Green, Clean Land, made of ten million bricks, five million alabaster mosaics, and a dome straight outta Xanadu, man, tiled troughs for horses, and riders, staircases of silver, a £14,000 window to keep out rough-sleeping celebrants, and a secret escape viaduct, 1,247 feet long for our Civic Leaders in time of public disorders. Swell, Ma, I dig that architecture, nuttin' delusional about it! Then the irredeemable Hogg rugurgitated the *Confessions of a Justified Sinner,* a very nasty innuendo book about goings on at the High Altar, a load of junk, really, about how awful God is. Bin it! God is grand, especially in a pulpit. But go outside too. Gaze at Eriskay, behold the Honours of Scotland, the Gaelic crown-jewel, buried next to the Art Decco Swimming Pool. Hearken to the thirty-six bells of Fife, admire the old snuff cottages, with their painted pantiles and perambulatory toilets. Now I went there to visit the most vital moveable feast in Pictland – the Cleopatra Needle of Crief, dedicated to the first distillery ever inaugurated here overnight. Forget the Fairisle woollies, Harris's Tweed, Lewis's hankies, have a dram in Aberdeen, famous for its Claret. Close by, it is said, Flora had another spasm with a dishevelled prince in one of Madame's crammed cubicles. Rumour and innuendo, I say, typical yellow froth. Ignore it! And still more shining Verdant Works rose up In Weegieland, with huge propellers, which refuse to take off, and, still outside, Abroath with its Abbey, outdoes all the sensational runic remains and awful new inventions I've mentioned. The Declaration of Abroath there, what beatific calligraphy! - the Pope raised his holy forefinger over it. Yes, yes, yes! Native independence for every NED in the land! 'Let me hold your ha...ha..ha...hand...' After all we are proud Dependants now, caloo callay, cowed to a woman, put that in your sporran and ignite it! No, I'm not confused about this. I have tremendous outbursts of crystal conviction, and lovely Lyn always said, 'to your own independence be true, and it will follow...' etc, etc... I have it noted. I am, and was am, Ally MacNally, now especially! Bastard fleas as busy as bees. *(Scratches wildly)* Yellow pubic con, ye celandine swine! But I impregnate this final fun costume even as I put it on. *(Sprays tattered costume)* There! There! There! All deceased, scratched out, erased from human conflict. Yellows thought they'd down us with flea-bites, did they? - never has one nation been so completely self-deluded by another! *(Shakes jacket)* See! Clouds of lemon-hued corpses. See 'em. Deceased and dead! Cummupances got at last, down the plughole, and so farewell, ye silly daffodil hoppers, offspring of flaxen Hengest and Horsa! Harbingers of colossal conceit ending in endless declines and falls, so shut the mum-humping up! Yes...lovely Lynn of Lore...

(Scots accent) And as the sun sets, see, from the quay, the millions of silver fish, the little darlings, from the Outer Hebrides sucked aboard by a giant vacuum hose, enough breakfasts for ten thousand Hairies on a picnic! And lots of Fishermen's Friends still hanging on. Then a final dip in the Caverns of the Great Scoop of Gruinard Bay or raw in the Black

Mullins or a final chat with the Old Man of Storr, guardian of the famous tartan boulder. As for lofty Ben Nevis – leave her to Heavens Above! Then gaze a little over the side and behold, again, the city under the waves, marvellous Brigadoon, and I don't mean the pissing Taff Avallon either. And don't forget those dozen brochures or so with the oats for breakfast. And as you wave farewell from the stern, fly with the puffins, kittiwarks, razor bills, fulmers, guillemots, sorry petrols, nasty terns, Nurse marauders, short-eared owls, golden plovers, high and mighty eagles, hen-harriers, pine martins, tons of shags, and behold, on the headlands, the giant Sea-Shells of Brodgar, the Pompey of the North! - with its message for all time, 'remember Dunegan! Fly the Flag of the great Clan Chief!' where I had my fiftieth-second sight, let alone reincarnation. Gaelic was spoken.

(Goes back stage, dresses in last bits of costume) Now, at the end, I tell you, I had you in the palm of my lagoon, didn't I? You believed every word. Well, grab your purses, here is the bleeding truth of life still alive in old Celtic lands, and the new one to come. Listen quick, I can hear the blond barbarians at the gates. And you wait, as soon as they hear I'm delivering my next message, received by conch-shell but a day ago, they'll be here with their tranquillizers, hypodermics, capsules, straitjackets, alien commandments and dirty postcards. See, on with my 70th lecture, my 78th Second Sightings, my hundredth reincarnation, O ye presbyters, confessors, professors, Covenanters, elders, saints and

sinners, however respectable, this is what I have worked and schemed for all my life, in here and out, ladies permitting, all the rest is mere subterfuge. Twenty-five of the old nations, all under one bed, what a commotion in these isles when this message gets out! Twenty eight. Together! It's alright Ma... Who am I to say? Me! That's who! Here it comes! Watch as I unfurl the flag, I reveal it at the very least. *(Unfurls saltire flag, on it is written, 'Remember Dunegan! Fight for Ally MacNally First Clan Chief Elect of all the Clans of our new Nova Scotia!' Flourishes flag)* I am Ally MacNally of the clan Ally MacNally, first Clan Chief Elect of all the clans of our New Nova Scotia, après referendum! Behold, lovely Lynn of Lorne, I am out now out and about, yes! - 'be ye what ye are, be a SCOT!' *(Gestures to map and brochures with pointer, as at opening)* So permit me to present to you – Scotland the Brave! *(Roars of rage, shouts, shots, jeers, chains clank, steel doors clang, shouted orders, ' Raus! Raus! Raus!' Stuka dive bombers, clash of arms, as at beginning. EXIT ALLY. CUT LIGHTS, SOUND. Snatch of Harry Lauder's 'Keep right on to the end of the road...' HOUSE LIGHTS UP)*

CURTAIN

Titles from Creative Print Publishing Ltd

Fiction

The Shadow Line & The Secret Sharer   Joseph Conrad
ISBN 978-0-9568535-0-9

Kristina's Destiny   Diana Daneri
ISBN 978-0-9568535-1-6

Andrew's Destiny   Diana Daneri
ISBN 978-0-9568535-2-3

To Hold A Storm   Chris Green
ISBN 978-0-9568535-3-0

Ten Best Short Stories of 2011   Various
ISBN 978-0-9568535-5-4

The Lincoln Letter   Gretchen Elhassani
ISBN 978-0-9568535-4-7

Dying to Live   Katie L. Thompson
ISBN 978-0-9568535-7-8

Keeping Karma   Louise Reid
ISBN 978-0-9568535-6-1

Escape to the Country   Patsy Collins
ISBN 978-0-9568535-8-5

Lindsey's Destiny   Diana Daneri
ISBN 978-0-9568535-9-2

ANGELS UNAWARES   Dedwydd Jones

ISBN 978-1-909049-02-4

RELICK   Steven Gepp
ISBN 978-1-909049-03-1

It Hides In Darkness   Ross C. Hamilton
ISBN 978-1-909049-04-8

Transmission of Evil   Mandy Sheering
ISBN 978-1-909049-06-2

Ransom   Don Nixon
ISBN 978-1-909049-07-9

Milwaukee Deep   G. Michael
ISBN 978-1-909049-05-5

PANDORA   Marcus Woolcott
ISBN 978-1-909049-09-3

Shadowscape The Stevie Vegas Chronicles   M. R. Weston
ISBN 978-1-909049-10-9

Alaric, Child Of The Goths   Daniel F. Bowman
ISBN 978-1-909049-08-6

For Catherine   Elizabeth Morgan
ISBN 978-1-909049-01-7

Black Book on the Welsh Theatre   Dedwydd Jones
ISBN 978-1-909049-11-6

MASKS or The Golden Omega   Dedwydd Jones
ISBN 978-1-909049-13-0
The Lazis Project   Marcus Woolcott
ISBN 978-1-909049-14-7

Hilarious Tales for Kids and Grown Ups   Dedwydd Jones
ISBN 978-1-909049-15-4

Nonfiction

Amazonia – My Journey Into The Unknown   -Adam Wikierski
ISBN 978-1-909049-00-0

Recollections of Pathos and the Greek Islands   Les Burgess
ISBN 978-1-909049-12-3

Contacting Creative Print Publishing Ltd

Creative Print Publishing are publishers of books covering various genres including all kinds of fiction, non-fiction and life histories.

For more details contact:

Creative Print Publishing Ltd
Creative Print Studios
Rear of No 7, Broomfield Road
Marsh
Huddersfield
HD1 4QD

United Kingdom

Web: http://www.creativeprintpublishing.com

Email: info@creativeprintpublishing.com Tel:

+44 (0) 1484 314 985

Lightning Source UK Ltd.
Milton Keynes UK
UKOW03f1320011213

222137UK00002B/91/P